I Speak

Portraits by Megan Wyeth

Interviews documented by Anthony Glise

SURREAL PORTRAITS AND INTERVIEWS WITH GUITARS FROM THE LAST 200 YEARS

— I Speak —
Surreal Portraits and Interviews with Guitars From the Last 200 Years

Copyright © 2017 by
Megan Wyeth and Anthony Glise
All Rights Reserved.

Library of Congress Cataloging-in-Publication Data:

Wyeth, Megan, 1956 - Anthony Glise, 1956 -
I Speak: Surreal Portraits and Interviews with Guitars from the Last 200 Years.
Megan Wyeth *(photography)* and Anthony Glise *(text, layout, and design).*
Official Publication Date: April 10, 2017.

Library of Congress Control Number: 2012905554
ISBN-10: 0-9854220-3-3
ISBN-13: 978-0-9854220-3-5

FOR MORE INFORMATION AND DETAILS ON PURCHASING
LIMITED-EDITION GALLERY PRINTS, POSTERS, AND CDs, CHECK
AMAZON.COM, OTHER ONLINE OUTLETS, OR CONTACT THE PUBLISHER:

Aevia Publications. Ltd.
P.O. Box 7242
St. Joseph, MO 64507 — USA
EMAIL: AEVIAGROUP@GMAIL.COM

Dedicated to our families and friends...

SOME FLESH AND BONE,
SOME WOOD AND GLUE.

— Megan & Anthony —

A SPECIAL THANKS to:

John W. Hans at *Dolphin Archival Printing,*
Thomas Ransom at *Ransomed Productions* for CD post-production and mastering.
Richard and Eric Coco of *LaBella String Company* (New York)
for gallery support and endorsement
and
Audio Technica Microphones (US) for gallery presentation sound support
and especially Roxanne for encouragement beyond the call of duty.

Contents

Portraits & Interviews
with Guitars by:

FOREWORD ——

I love the idea of "reincarnated voices" of the instruments talking to us "in the now." *Very* uplifting, ancient, and justified. *Beautiful* pictures by the madam! You have my blessings for your book.

It's a gem!

Jan Akkerman
Dutch Rock Guitar Legend
Former lead guitarist with "Focus"

After reading this unexpectedly unique book, I realized I was able to add my human words to the language I was reading as *"Guitar."*

Before this book existed, I thought guitars were only *"gently weeping."* But after reading it, I decided to listen in a different way to each note my guitar "said." And it appears Anthony is definitely correct: *my guitar speaks.* In a weird mix of French and "Guitar" *but she definitely speaks! And I'm honored to be her current "Person."*

This book is not only a wonderful source of information about old and precious instruments, but a true piece of art.

Bravo to Anthony for his unusual and clever contribution to classical guitar literature and to the talented photographer, Megan Wyeth, for her photography!

Roland Dyens
Classical Guitarist and Composer, Professor, Conservatoire National Supérieur de Musique de Paris - France

This is a delicate, beautiful and original book in which guitars are really the protagonists, and they not only give us their sound, but also their feelings and thoughts.

Amalia Ramírez de Galarreta
Owner, Ramírez Guitar Company— Madrid, Spain

What a beautiful book, and what a beautiful idea for a book! As musicians, we expect our favorite instruments to "speak" to us, but sometimes we have to listen more carefully to truly hear all that they can tell us.

The "old-timers," especially, often have extraordinary personal histories of travel, purpose, performance, and sometimes neglect and rebirth.

Frank Koonce
Professor of Music, Arizona State University

We enjoyed the originality of your approach to the book and the photos are beautiful. We wish you lots of success! Best wishes,

David and María Russell
Classical Guitarist & Recording Artist

A touching book. It strikes a chord... *or several.*

Joel Cohen, *Music Director Emeritus, The Boston Camerata*

This is an unusual yet captivating read. I love the photography and the interesting text. However, what really intrigued me was the extremely creative use of type.

A pleasure to peruse!

William Bay
Chairman of the Board, Mel Bay Publications

What a delightful suite of surprises! Thank you both for giving voice, vision, and character to these lovely instruments.

Thomas Heck, Ph.D.
Founding Member, Guitar Foundation of America

I enjoyed Mr. Glise's playful personification of these instruments by these great guitar luthiers. It is a light-hearted and fun read, and the photographs by Ms. Wyeth are really great.

Jason Vieaux
Classical Guitarist
Faculty, Curtis Institute of Music, Cleveland Institute of Music
1st Prize Winner, GFA Competition (1992)

As musicians, we never own the instruments we play, we are merely their caretakers over our lifespan. In their wonderfully surprising new book, *I Speak,* Megan and Anthony have documented not only how their beloved instruments have matured during their "watch," but how these instruments have in turn transformed them as musicians and artists.

One can only hope that the future caretakers of our instruments will be as observant and considerate.

Ben Verdery
Classical Guitarist, Chair, Guitar Department, Yale University

"Anthony and Megan have created a charming book about the outward shapes and inner lives of guitars. Beautifully photographed, artfully designed, and sensitively written, this book uses exquisite images and imaginative monologues *(really, brief prose poems)* to grasp the unique personality of each instrument. Some of the guitars here are brash, some are meditative, and one has been so traumatized, she is all but mute. Yet each piece, each instrument, offers us a distinct perspective on music, history, experience. *It's a pleasure to see and to listen to them all."*

Glenn Kurtz, *author of*
"Practicing: A Musician's Return to Music"

Encounters of a highly original kind, Anthony brings us the historical, emotional and humoristic sides of his faithful companions. Megan's pictures artistically reveal *"les coins cachés"* of each instrument! **Listen, admire, and enjoy!**

Ken Sugita
Concert Violinist-French National Orchestra-Lille

Preface —

FAR FROM the ubiquitous documentaries of guitars, the gallery exhibition and book, *I Speak*, is about some of my dearest friends; the experiences, quirks, joys, and sorrows of their lives:

— the rage at watching Napoléon's attack of Vienna,
—the fear of being left in a 19th-century barbershop,
—the quiet joy of being a mother,
—the nervous excitement of playing in Carnegie Hall,
—and the terrified disgust at the Nazi rampage
*   through the city streets during "Kristalnacht."*

After long discussions with the guitars, Megan's photos captured these personalities.

SOME OF THEM (particularly the females) were *quite* insistent on only allowing photos that showed their best features: erotic curves, sensual complexions, or flowing neck lines, while some (mostly the males) were adamant on touting their battle scars and bravura.

MY INTERVIEWS with them became very personal and surprisingly confidential *exposés* that can only happen when a guitar feels comfortable enough to let down the defenses and speak openly *(a trait that is irrationally threatening to many of us!).*

SOME OF THE INSTRUMENTS were quietly reserved—waiting patiently for *(as they call us)* "their Person" to have them repaired so they can sing again.

OTHERS ARE ACTIVE concert or recording artists whose pride, confidence, and ego were nearly impossible to contain!

THEY SPEAK

- and speak clearly -

to anyone who has the patience to listen as Megan and I have done—*as perhaps we should all do with each other*—because, as the guitar "Antonella" gently reminds us in her interview,

> "… AFTER ALL -
>   YOU,
>   ME,
>   AND THE REST OF US…?
>
>   …WE'RE ONLY HUMAN."

Anthony Glise
Sainghin-en-Mélantois, France
Winter, 2017

Megan Wyeth —

- studied with Ansel Adams (at ages 18-19)
- additional studies with Arnold Newman
- workshops including *Sante Fe Photographic Workshops, Society for Contemporary Photography, Kansas City Art Institute*
- arts outreach and educational programs
- solo exhibits throughout the US
- 4 featured books of photography
- mediums including alternative processes, polaroid transfer, & diverse subject matter
- contributor to numerous books, publications, and exhibitions

further details at: **www.MeganWyeth.com**

— Anthony Glise

- over 60 books and musical editions
- only American guitarist to win 1st Prize, *International Toscanini Competition* (Italy)
- concerts at *Carnegie Hall, Lincoln Center, Vienna International Center, Nouveau Siècle* (French National Orchestra), *et al.*
- recordings for *Dorian Recordings, Young Recording Artists* (US), *AME* (France), and *HEM* (Hungary)
- 30-year veteran duo partner with violinist, Ken Sugita, *French National Orchestra-Lille* (THE SUGITA/GLISE DUO)

further details at: **www.AnthonyGlise.com**

Portraits
&
Interviews

GOTTLIEB FISCHER
NAMED "MICHAEL"
(BORN CA. 1802)
VIENNA, AUSTRIA

I Remember Praying

that I would find my Person

and you know, honest prayers *are* answered

> **…BUT IT'S THE SMELL OF WALNUTS THAT I REMEMBER MOST.**

Back in my day, they'd crush the walnut husks, boil them down, and the barber would spread the thick mixture over men's hair to hide the gray.

You might laugh at that *now*, but it's no stranger than some of the things **you** people do today...

facelifts...?

hair implants... ?

Come now... I'm sorry, but I would have thought that the pride and ego of you people might have settled just a *little* through the years...

BUT I SUPPOSE WE **ALL** WANT TO MAKE OURSELVES MORE ATTRACTIVE, *no?*

And my **piercing?** It's really no worse than getting a pierced ear, you know?

Not a big deal.
A lot of us had them back then.

They would make a hOle in our head stock
at the top so they could
hang us by a ribbon
from a hook set
deeply in a
wall

which **I** must admit,
was *quite* practical!

Some of us were hung in
cafés, some in **bars**...
some of us

— *LIKE ME* —

were hung on the walls
of a **BARBERSHOP**
— *just left there* —

- hanging - until a customer,
*tired of waiting to have his face scraped
with a nearly sharp razor,*
would look up and notice.

— just hanging there by the ribbon.

My Person took me straight to his barbershop and hung me with my back against the cold wall

where I stayed
for
two
days.

Alone.
— Quiet —

I wasn't MADE to be quiet, you know?

And I was <u>bored</u>
AND a little
frightened

Then it happened.

A **fat** man he was - with gray hair (and honestly, so *little* hair
that I wondered why he was in a barbershop!)

but he must have been tired of waiting
for his shave or maybe he wanted to
have his hair colored dark brown
with the rich, thick walnut oil.

I REALLY DON'T RECALL.

He kept glancing at me during a rant about the price of eggs.

Finally
— slowly —

the conversation lagged — *and he stood up.*

He walked toward me and plucked me from the wall.

*He had such a **friendly** smile!*

He sat with me, held me close,
and strummed a few chords.
Nothing profound, you know?

Just some Alpine folk song,
but it felt so good to *sing* and
I could *tell* he had played before
and even as simple as his song was,
everyone in the barbershop stopped

for a moment
···*silence*···

They listened.
He let me sing — and EVERYONE smiled.
Then he carefully hung me

back
on
the
wall.

They turned **LOUD** again; *talking, laughing — waiting —*
for their turn to be shaved, or clipped,
or have their gray hair
colored so that their

girlfriends,
WIVES *lovers*
OR

might find them more

attractive.

Funny...

I wonder if any of them
realized that **ALL** they
needed to do

. was to *hold me —*
sing *with me...*

and it would have made them

just as attractive
to their women.

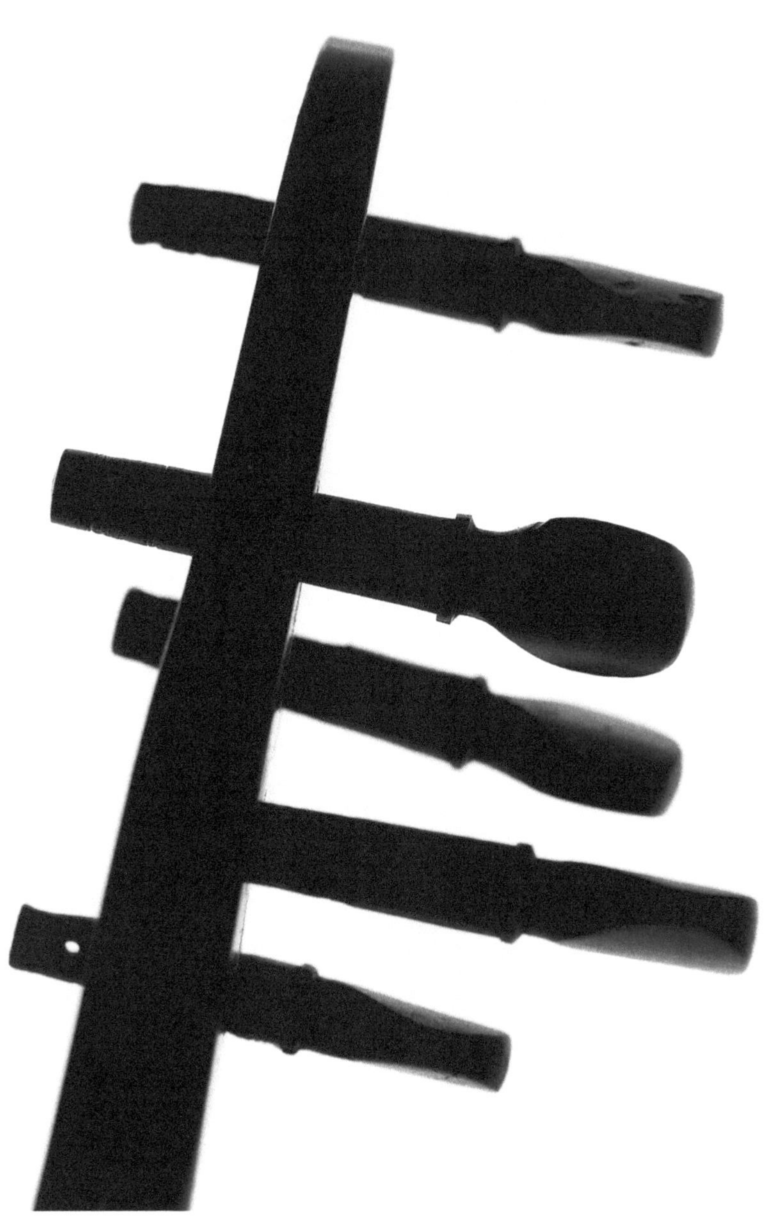

Isn't it strange?

When we sing, we are *all*

– every one of us –

more beautiful!

And wasn't it St. Augustine who said,
"𝔥e who sings, prays twice"?

So there you have it... it's no wonder my prayers were answered.
*They were **HONEST** prayers*

— AND

I sing.

But all that aside...

...IT'S THE SMELL OF THE WALNUTS
THAT I REMEMBER MOST.

Anonymous
Named "Constance"
(born ca. 1814)
Vienna, Austria [?]

Many of **you** think of us as
women
and,

like me,

many of us *are* female.

It's not *vanity*,
I suppose it's the *shape* —
the **long** slender neck
AND *graceful figure* –

but of course without the need of a **BRA** or those
"CONTROL-TOP PANTYHOSE"

that so many of you think are necessary
to keep your fleshy bumps under submission.

No —

Our *figures* are just part of who we are
and <u>we</u> accept it...

*which **perhaps** is something
you might learn from us, eh?*

I **can** be a little testy sometimes -

maybe that goes with my gender.

If you don't treat me right,
I simply won't react the way you expect — ***or want*** —

>   but if you hold me gently,
>   caress me, tease me (BUT NOT TOO MUCH),
>   I'll let you coax ANY sound out of me
>   that I have to give.

Giving is what we were ALL made to do, *you know?*

I'M NOT SO DIFFERENT
FROM YOU.

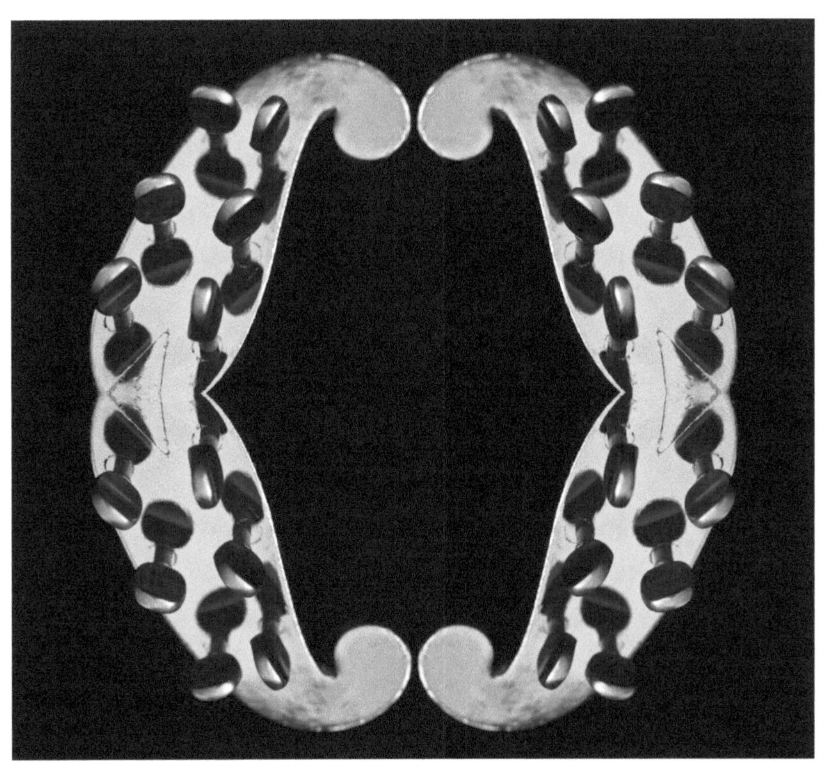

You **love,**

 marry,
AND GIVE THE WORLD

 children

who eventually leave you
to start that cycle
all over again.

I give you *sound,*
and like your children,

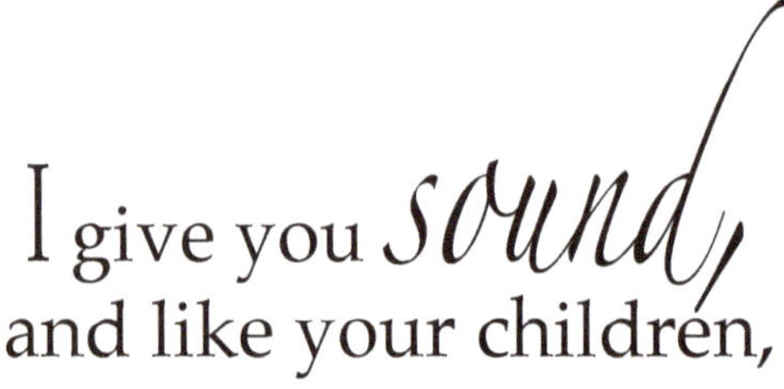

that SOUND leaves me,
takes on it's own life,
and touches someone else.

You see... ?
we're *not* so different...

except,

of course,

for that **ABSURDITY**
of your undergarments!

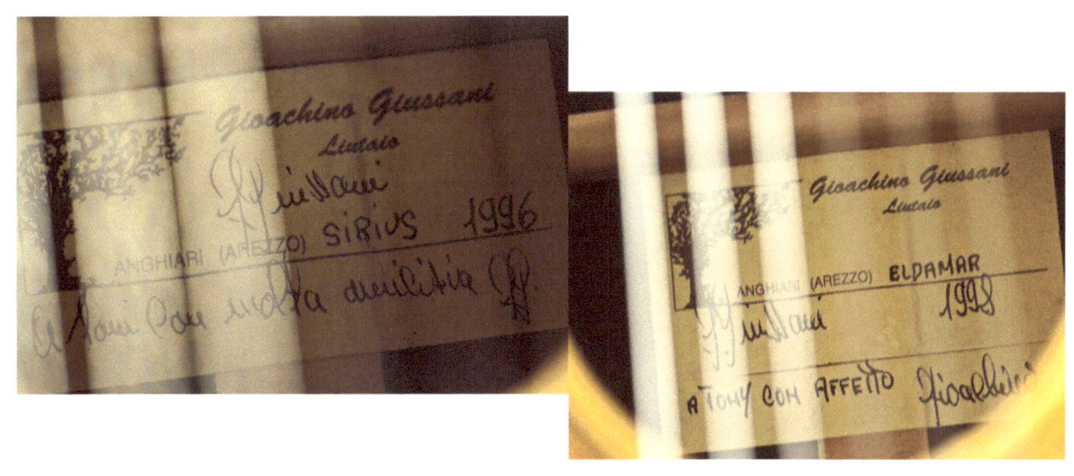

GIOACHINO GIUSSANI
NAMED "SIRIUS"
(BORN 1996)
ANGHIARI, AREZZO, ITALY

Each of us has a rôle…

My little brother was made only for concerts.

He's **LOUD** - *most little brothers are, you know?*
Blusterous —
and sometimes a little out of control…

Me ?

I was made <u>only</u> for recording.

Of course I'm beautiful

enough to catch your eye on stage,

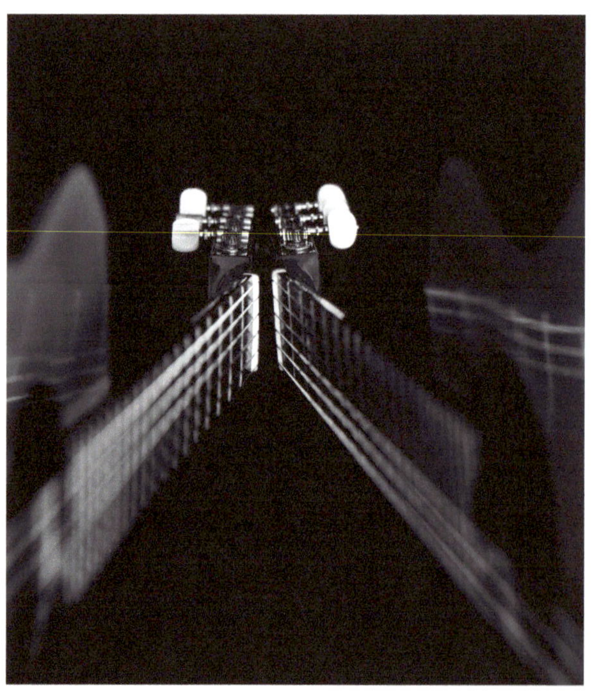

but I'm a bit like a quiet, *exquisite* painting,

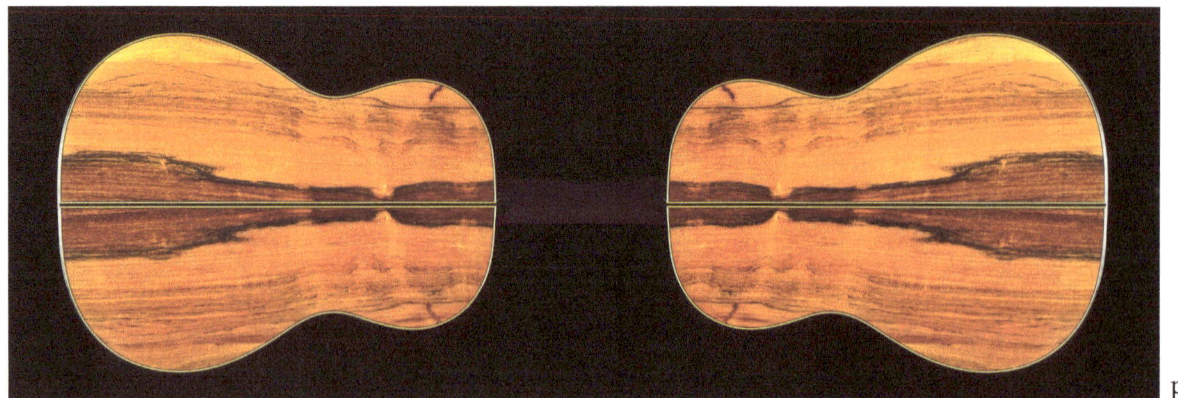

hung in the dark sacristy of an old church.

A painting that only the priest sees each Sunday as he slowly, meticulously, prepares for mass.

I don't care.

Stage lights blind me,
I _don't_ like crowds

— *AND* —

being tucked away in
a flight case so some

idiot

baggage handler
doesn't destroy me
on the way to the
next concert,

WELL…

I'm a bit introverted and I won't FORCE my ideas on anyone,
but if you know how to talk with me, I'll give you *any* sound you want.

Any sound.

With the *slightest* tip of the right hand

I can give you a
totally different color
on *every* single note
in *every* single position,

and my volume is *perfectly* balanced for the most *sensitive* microphone —

MY PERSON'S PRODUCER *LOVES* ME FOR THAT!

My strings are set **very low,** SO YOU CAN'T OVERPLAY ME LIKE YOU CAN A CONCERT GUITAR.

You see?

all of us have a rôle; one that we were made for. I hope you find yours because

your place in life can be difficult to find and it's often not at ALL what you thought it would be, you know? *But as for me?*

I was made for color and you'll *never* find me on stage, but you can hear me sing on recordings and sometimes a radio or television show.

That's my rôle—and let me tell you something,

I sing — *and I do it well!*

– NATURALLY

I don't recall when I was born,
any more than **you** remember
that moment when you fell from
grace —

thrust from your mum's
tummy into a world of bright
lights, cold hard air, and a room
full of impossibly tall strangers,

POKING AND PRODDING to make
sure your entrance onto
this stage of life would
be as safe as possible.

There's *SO* much I don't
remember,

BUT I'D WAGER YOU'VE
FORGOTTEN A LOT TOO, NO?

My head, body, and braces were carved *flawlessly*.

My sides and back are maple -
a bit unstable, but *beautiful!*

They were cut,
shaved, steamed,
bent, and set with
a spruce top so not
a *seam* would show.

ABSOLUTELY PERFECT!

The fretting jarred me a little -
carefully pounding the strips of

German silver

into my fingerboard
at just the right places
so I would play in tune,

BUT OUR FRETTING IS PROBABLY NO
DIFFERENT THAN YOU GETTING
YOUR FIRST SHOT AT THE
DOCTOR'S OFFICE.

WE ALL SURVIVE THOSE
LITTLE **JABS OF LIFE, DON'T WE?**

I remember the lacquer was **warm** when my Maker
spread it over me;

that was my favorite!

It was *comforting* - I suppose like the embryonic fluid
washing over you during *your* birth

...which I bet
you don't remember either.

ISN'T IT SAD ──────────────────────────────
THAT WE'VE FORGOTTEN ALL THAT ?
...THE "BIRTH ?"

But those memories,
ABANDONED ON UTERINE SHORES,

don't diminish the joy
that the others must
have felt to be in
the room when
we made our
debuts

— and that
merciful amnesia
certainly doesn't
negate the
miracle
of our existence!

WE'VE ALL GONE THROUGH IT

AND WE'VE ALL FORGOTTEN.

NOW, as I said,
maple is *beautiful*
but unstable;
"...the spirit is willing but the flesh is weak," and all that.

Your blonds **sunburn** easily,
some of you have bad **teeth**
and some of you need **glasses**.

**WE'RE ALL PREDISPOSED
TO A FRAGILITY
THRUST ON US BY AGE.**

I have maple sides and back - with so many curls in the grain -
and at every *curl*, the wood is weaker
and has the potential to crack...
and I did, BUT FACE IT...

how do you think **YOU'RE**
going to look in 200 years?

Like you —
I'll be fixed someday
when my Person has
the time and money.

I'll go through a rebirth.

Probably not as traumatic
as the first one,
but I'll remember it *all*
next time . . .

just as surely as
you'll remember your
gentle passing

from
this life

to the next.

Hermann Hauser, Jr.
Named "Wilhelm"
(born 1971)
Munich, Germany

THERE IS SO MUCH TALK ABOUT FOREIGNERS TODAY!

This group is welcome, this one isn't;
this one fits in,
this one doesn't;
this one's a different color;
this one has a different religion, eats strange food, AND

...*this* one doesn't speak English... like God does...!

I SOMEHOW THINK THE ALMIGHTY CAN MANAGE DIFFERENT VERB CONJUGATIONS – *ACCENTS* –

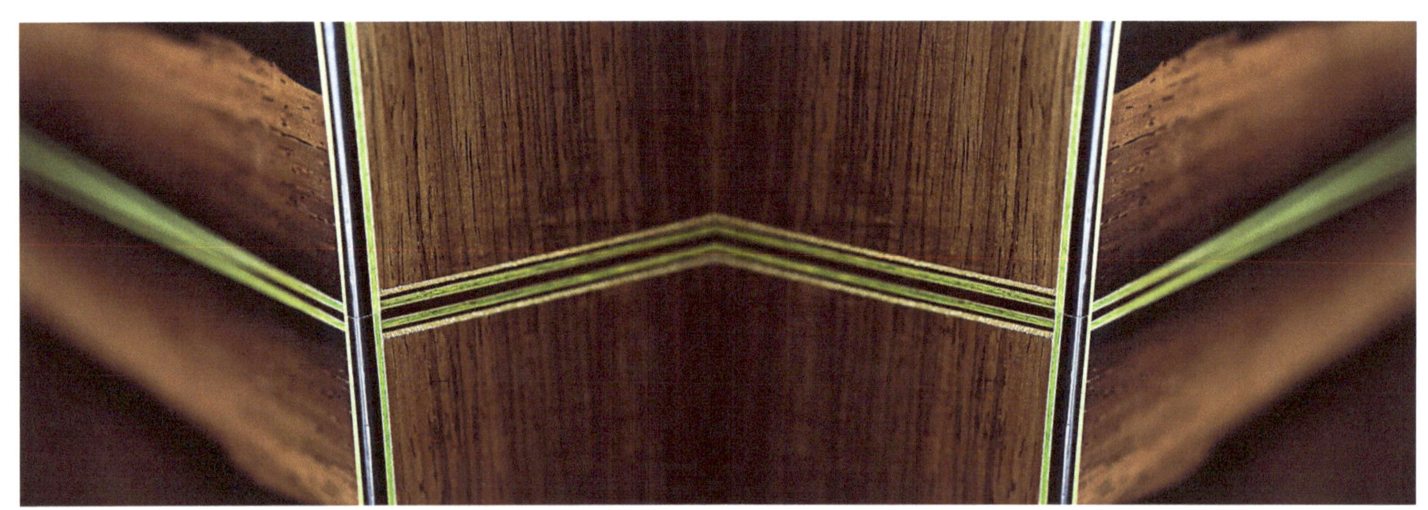

and **my heavy German dialect.**

Quatsch... Nonsense...

Have you forgotten that Jesus himself was multi-lingual ?
— Hebrew — Aramaic — even some Greek.
He was probably quite dark, middle-eastern looking,

AND... *Jesus didn't fit in.*

Immigration versus integration?

That's absurd.

YOU WANT TO KNOW WHAT A <u>FOREIGNER</u> IS?

It's someone brave enough to leave everything they ever knew and loved.

Someone who had the courage to leave a father and mother to try and find something different

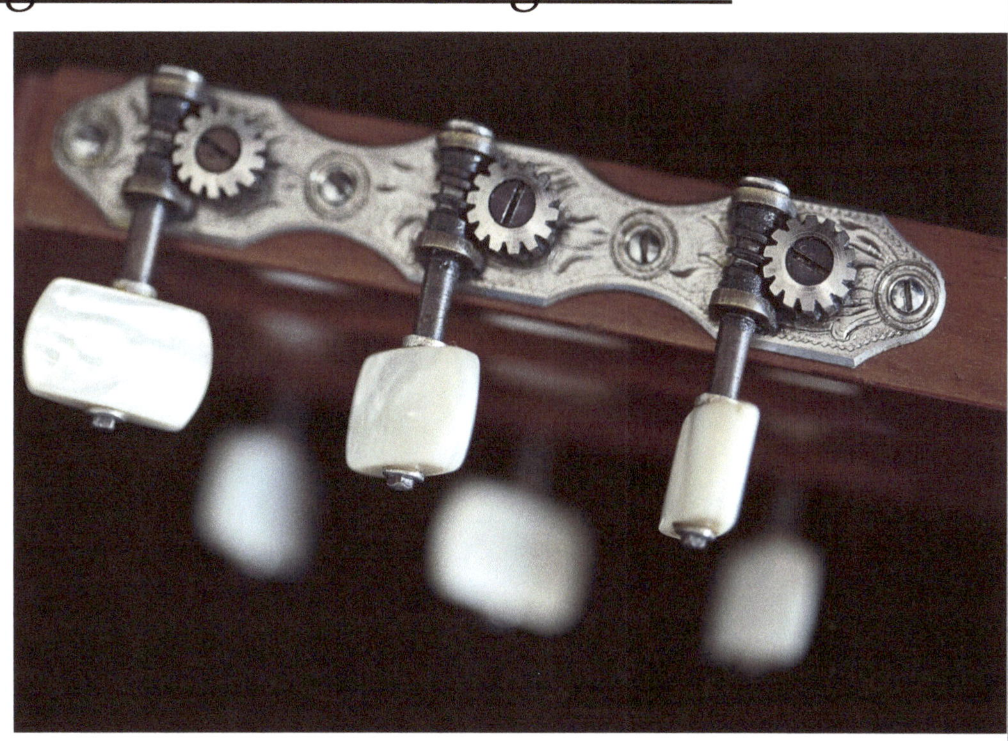

- *something **better** -*
and *yes*, I did it
and *no*, I didn't "fit in."

It's easy to forget that countries are renewed
by people who left, or were kicked out
of every other decent country on
earth and it's easy to forget that

CONSERVATIVES WORSHIP DEAD RADICALS.

I have a light colored spruce top; VERY unpopular at the time!

I'm German *(Spanish guitars were <u>much</u> more welcomed back then)* *and* I didn't speak the language:
cedar tops have a rich, dark tone color that most guitars spoke back then,
but cedars can mask the subtly of a phrase.
Spruces like me speak clearly — distinctly —
but with an accent.

Still, in my day,
CEDARS were the "accepted" foreigners.
The spruces, like *me?*

I might as well have been made out of plywood.

Yes, I'm PROUD of my heritage, but at the same time I'm PROUD of my *new* home.

Most foreigners feel like that.

Your grandfather or great grandfather knew that AND IF YOU'VE FORGOTTEN,
I think it's a little sad.

Our past is part of who we all are.
Our past is part of the glorious diversity
that we bring to every new home
that we claim as our own…

…but *mench,*

NOW AND THEN…
I *do* miss a good Dunkles Weissen Bavarian beer!

Prosit !

Kenny Hill
Named "Jayden"
(born 2009)
Ben Lomond, USA

OK ! So what *NOW* ?
Let's get moving, OK? *YEAH !*

I think we should do a concert -
like - just **CALL** somebody!
Now, ok? Really!

- I MEAN **NOW** -
**I *REALLY* want to do
a *concert!***

Hey - I wanna play in *Carnegie Hall,* OK ?
Let's **do** it, *OK?*

...and that scale -
let's get that *happenin'* OK **?**
Faster - just speed *up* -
it's cool -

I can take it!

Just *DO* it, ok?

Come on! Yeah! **YEAH ! ! !**
Uh... *arpeggios...???*
Wanna do some arpeggios?
Let's do some arpeggios ! ! !
I *love* arpeggios!
REALLY luv'em!

They *tickle,* ya know?

I kinda like...

— oooh *yeah*

*oooooooooooo*h YEAH!!!!

F - SHARP !

F-sharp! Man! Check - it - *out* !
I *love* that note!
Listen to my *F-sharp* ! ! !

**Man, have I got a *killer* F-sharp
or <u>WHAT ???</u>**

Oh, *OH...* check THIS out!
Check out my **E major chord** !
You *ever* heard an E Major chord

 *that full???*

M*an, I am* Sooooooo <u>ON!!!!!</u>

Oh -OK -hey, HEY… try some BACH on me! *Check this out!*

- Listen to my LINES! *I mean,*

com'ON

Dude!

"YOU'RE NEW
and
YOU'RE A SPRUCE-TOP."

"WE HAVE TO BREAK YOU IN

— *gently* —

OR YOU'LL GET
HOT SPOTS."

oooooooh…

MAN…

BUMMER…

Franz Herzlieb, Sr.
Named "Alma"
(born ca. 1817)
Graz, Austria

I _am_ a special one!

Of course we **all** feel like that, but you can tell how much an old lady like **me** was appreciated with one little glance at my fingerboard!

Some of us

sang with professionals and our frets wore evenly up and down the neck,

but not me!

My Person only knew a few chords

down in first position.

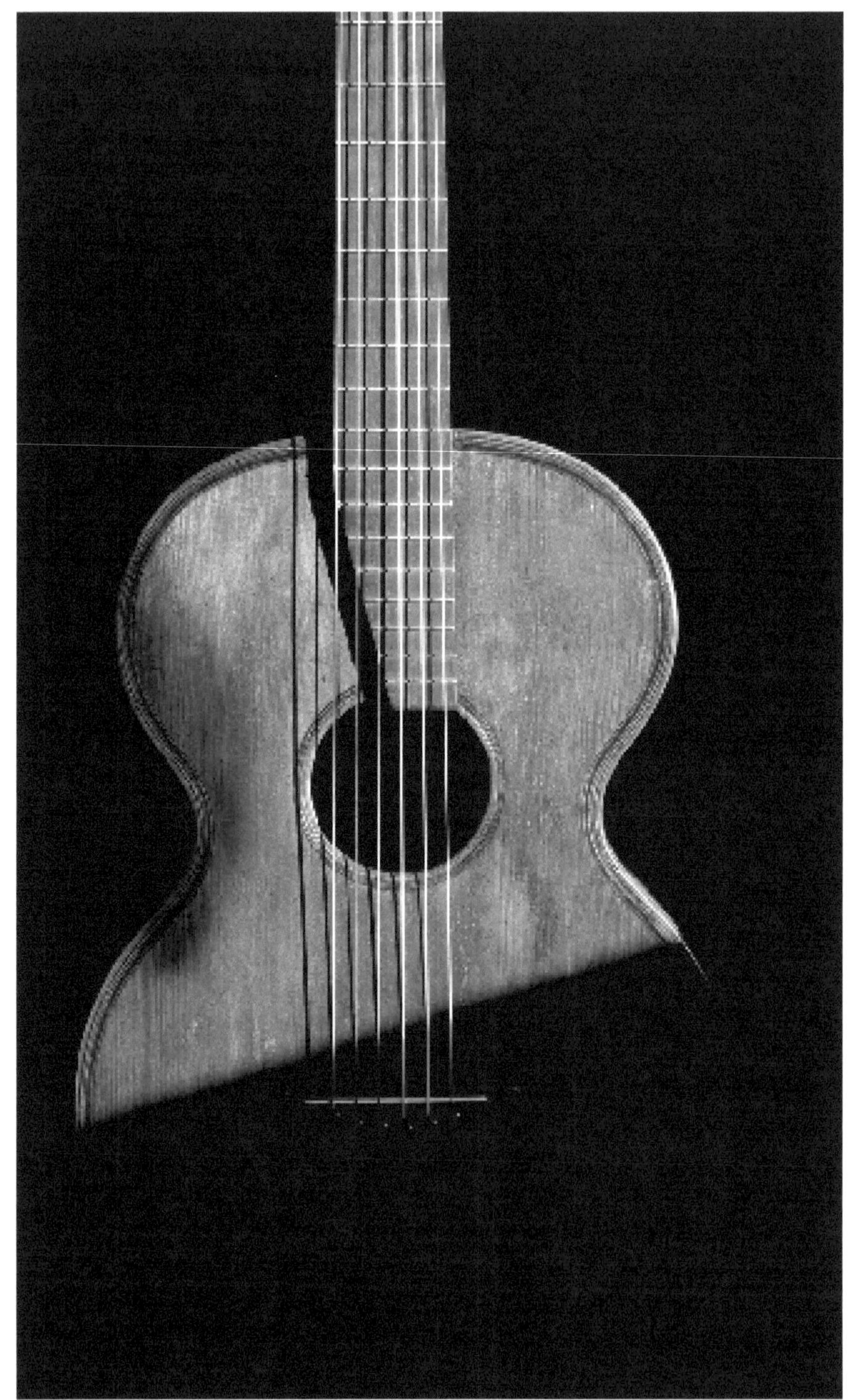

That's where I show *my* age.

You can see, where thousands of times,
she would play a G chord, a D, or an A

*(every once in a while she'd try that B minor chord…
but bar chords <u>always</u> gave her trouble!).*

No… almost everything *we* sang was in first position -
and my frets show that love - *but only there.*

Further up my neck, I'm just as *pristine*
as the DAY I was born!

I'M LIKE AN OLD GRANDMOTHER WHOSE HANDS, **through the years,**
HAVE STARTED TO SHOW THE INDISCRIMINATE SEVERITIES OF LIFE:

…the terror of watching
a brother go off to war…

…rocking a fragile child
with a fever that won't break,

…OR JUST THE DAILY
*"…gott'a get dinner
ready by 8 o'clock!"*

Hands mercilessly
show the age with you all,
but **forget** *the hands;*

that same wrinkled old
grandmother can have
the blissful smile of a
5-year old:

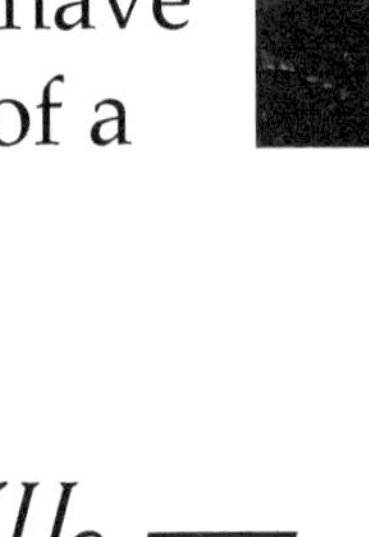

bright
— *JOYFUL* —

*unscathed by the anger, fear, or
just the tedious aspects of "living"
that eventually wear us* **ALL** *down.*

Some of my frets still glisten like new—

some are worn —

but deep inside,

I <u>*shine*</u>.

Lord... I *shine!*

That, my dear, is what makes us *all* special. No?
I hope you shine today.
I <u>really</u> do.

Now, wouldn't that be nice?

KARL HÖFNER
NAMED "DANIEL"
(BORN 1968)
BUBENREUTH, GERMANY

— My first Person thought that if he simply *bought* me, he could *play* me.

—NOTHING

IF YOU PRACTICE <u>NOTHING</u>

IS WHAT YOU GET BACK.
THAT HAPPENS TO A LOT OF US.

There's no **magic wand,** no **DEEP DARK SECRETS,** and I certainly can't play myself.

You can play only after you've earned the <u>RIGHT</u> to play and that right comes *ONLY* by work.

I was orphaned a few months after my first Person took me home.

Shut away in my case

in a closet until *that* got too full and I was cloistered on the back porch.

OVER A YEAR IN THE SUN, RAIN, SNOW…

You have a lot of time to think when you're all alone in the dark, BUT SOLITUDE can teach a host of virtues:

- you can rarely be proud
when you're alone,

you can't
argue with
anyone when
you're alone,

you learn your own
voice is not *nearly* as
interesting as another's,

and

**- BEING ALONE -
IS _NOT_ THE SAME
AS BEING LONELY.**

Eventually, even my **tiny**
space on the porch
was too much.

I was listed for sale
and my new Person
found me from that
newspaper ad.

FRANKLY - I THINK HE
BOUGHT ME OUT OF PITY -

but I've done the best I can for him
since he took me home.

We sing all different styles —
a little classical, jazz, folk, rock...
and he uses me when he composes.

You see... ?

*Patience is the salve of sorrow
and Work, the tool of success.*

I had *patience* -

my new Person *works*

and

I'm home now.
I **sing** *now!*

My finish cracked horribly from the elements in those early years, *but you know something…?*

I honestly don't *want* to be refinished.

NOT ONE OF US IS PERFECT AND EVERY ONE OF OUR FLAWS IS A RETICENT MANIFESTO OF HOW GOOD LIFE CAN BE.

I love my imperfections...

EVERY crack in my finish is truly a hairline furrow in a secluded path that led me to my <u>new</u> Person.

Gioachino Giussani
named "Eldamar"
(born 1998)
Anghiari, Arezzo, Italy

Life is a series of concert premieres.

That's all it is and my first at Carnegie Hall was <u>**MONUMENTAL.**</u>

<u>Naturally</u> I was a bit nervous but I was old enough to know

- and wise enough to trust -

that my Person **knew** what he was doing, and, I must say, we *were* well prepared.

We went out into the warmth of the stage lights with *such* confidence that everyone in the concert hall knew they were going to hear something *amazing.*

Pardon my narcissism.

<u>**THEY DID.**</u>

A few pieces by **Bach** (I've always loved Bach!),

some **Giuliani, Tárrega,**
and one of my Person's original pieces called
Dream Scenes;

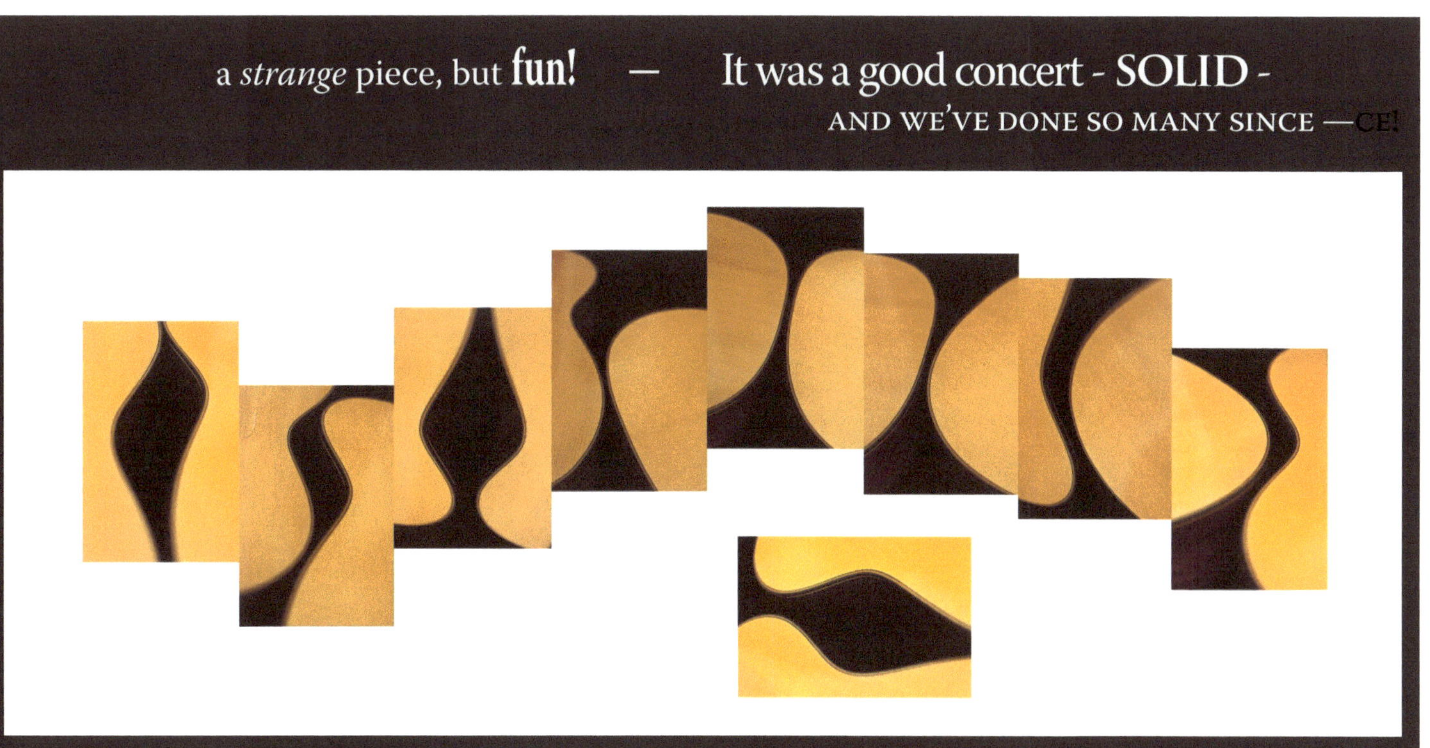

but somehow... *each* concert is a premiere.

ALL of us have those "PREMIÈRES"
throughout life,
you know?

They can be <u>LITTLE</u> things...

the summer's first lick of your favorite ice cream
while you're standing barefoot on a burning sidewalk;

when I sing a fast scale
and every note dances out of me
flawlessly.

When you watch the winter's first delicate
snowflake meander through the air
and perch

intentionally

on the edge of a tiny petal
of the last rose of the season

(MORE INTENTIONALLY THAN YOU HUMANS WOULD EVER BELIEVE!),

or the feeling I get from a fresh new set of strings being carefully tuned up to pitch.

Or they can be <u>BIG</u> things...

your very first day of school
when you're so excited that you can barely catch your breath.

The moment when you realize
that you've just met your
one true love,

or holding the hand of that person
who has been with you
— FOR WHAT SEEMS LIKE ETERNITY —
as they quietly drift from this life
and you hear that final breath
- *the last one that they will ever take*

— peacefully   leaving   their   body.

It's just a series of premieres
...isn't it?
Each one is
new,
exciting,
and sometimes
a little terrifying,
but I think that's OK.

It's just part of the plan.

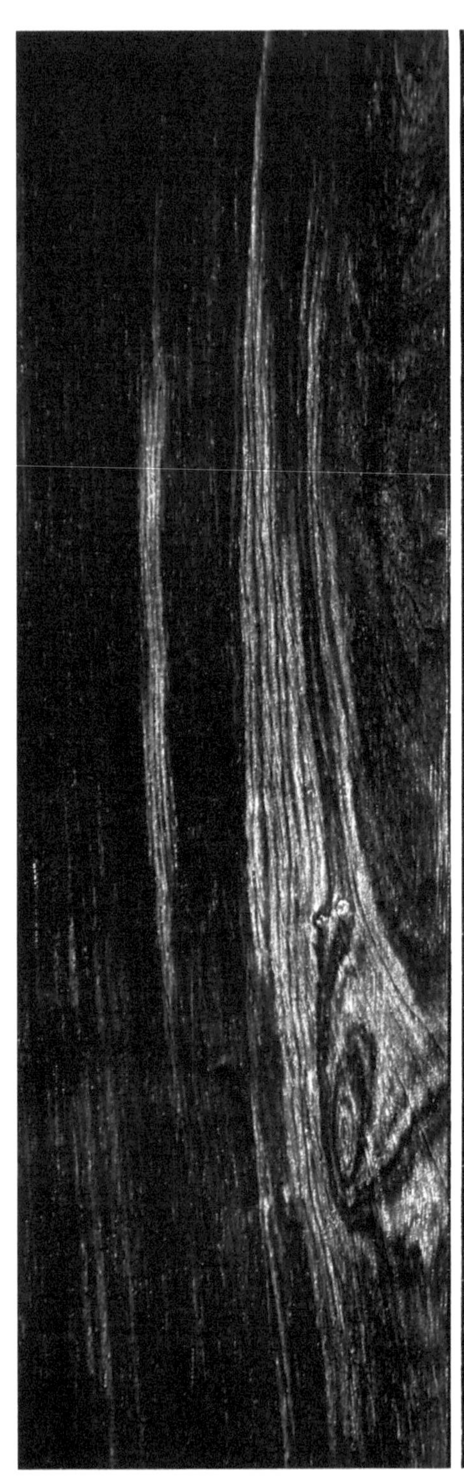

Your **Great Maker**
knew that

— **just as my Maker did** —

so you might as well accept it.

Each concert begins

— ENDS —

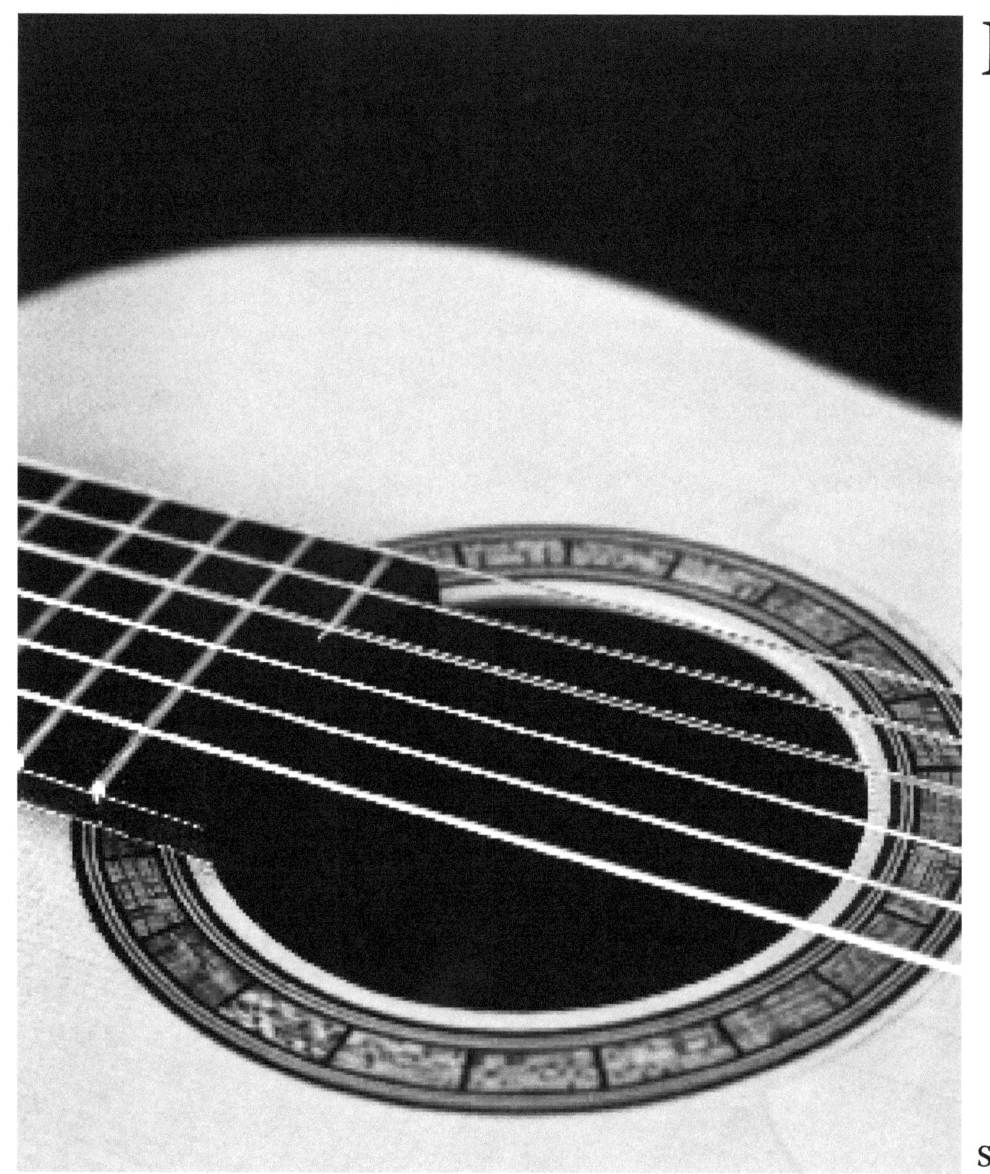

AND YOU MOVE

ON TO THE NEXT

with the applause
still ringing in your ears

**AND THE ADRENALINE
STILL TEARING THROUGH YOUR SOUL.**

Ferdinand Hell
Named "Maria"
(born ca. 1810's)
Vienna, Austria

— Ferdinand Hell

A Note from Anthony:

Ferdinand Hell was a highly respected Viennese maker in the early 19th century.

*Only a handful
of his children
still survive.*

THIS YOUNG LADY

was horribly abused
through the years
and has been so
emotionally
wounded
that she

can

barely

speak.

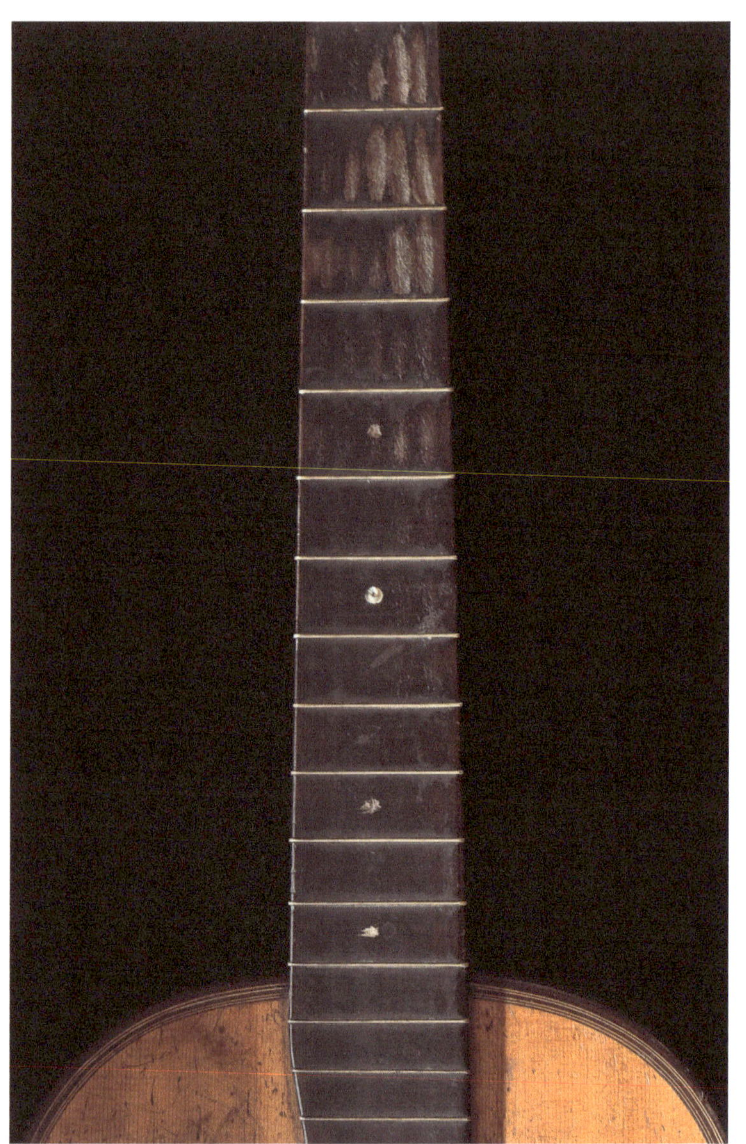

The *only* words I could gently coax from her were,

"…some of your People will understand."

H‍OW WE TREAT OTHERS
can have <u>SUCH</u> a profound affect on their lives.

We need to remember this.

José Ramírez
Named "Diego Manuel Aurelio"
(born 2008)
Madrid, Spain

Lineage?

Old families,
old money,
the sins of the father
to the sins of the son...?

Sorry to break it to you.

It doesn't work like that.

We <u>all</u> have a past that we have inherited
and we all have to overcome both
the good and bad of that
fabricated curse.

My Maker is the great grandson of old José Ramírez.

We've lived for centuries in Madrid
and there's probably not a classical
guitarist alive who hasn't played
one of my brothers or sisters, and
everyone knows our family tree.

I remember stories of the **proud** young man who wandered into
our shop asking to "rent" a guitar for a concert he had
<u>*that evening.*</u>

The builders in the shop laughed
"...a stupid request!"

Still, after listening to the young man play,
my Maker was so amazed
that he simply *GAVE* him the guitar!

That was the first time young **Andrés Segovia**
played a Ramírez in concert!

Llobet, Pujol, Presti, Ghiglia, Parkening, Williams, Bream, Pieri, Russell, Masters, Kanengiser, Tennant, Papandreou, Dyens, Leisner, Avers, Verdery, Vidović, Vieaux, York, THE **Assads,** THE **Romeros** - Pepe & the whole family...

AS I SAID,
THERE'S NOT A PLAYER ALIVE
WHO DOESN'T know our linage, but you ask what I have to say about me

— and my family…?

You know,

sometimes there's not a lot to say
because we just never take the time to notice!

LET ME ASK **YOU** -

What was your grandfather's favorite joke?

What did your mother cook the first time
she made a meal for your father?

When was the first time you saw
your sister laugh?
…your brother cry?
…what was the very first
song that you ever sang?

You see?

There are some things, so little,
YET **SO** IMPORTANT AND PERSONAL, **that they** quietly

- discreetly -

become part of who we are,
but we don't ever pay enough attention at that moment to *realize* it!

I'M NOT FANCY, but I have a solid,

"real" sound with bracing
and structure like the old ones in my family.

I'm *PART* of that family -
*but is that **all** I am?*

Yes - I have "Linage"
BUT I AM <u>SO</u> MUCH MORE!

Like you,
I am <u>ME</u>...

responsible for my *own* Lineage

— my *own* glories —

<u>AND</u> my own sins.

Johann Georg Staufer
named "Antonella"
(born ca. 1800)
Vienna, Austria

I'M PROUD
THAT I SURVIVED.

Not without a few scars, but by Mercy or by Grace,
I survived it all.

Yes, I know, Pride is one of the
"Seven Deadly Sins"

(and trust me,
born in a country
as **Catholic** as Austria,
you _learn_ **Church Dogma!**)

but it's a little hard to _not_ be proud when you've seen

- AND SURVIVED -
all that I have.

There are only SIX
like me still alive.

I have a sister who
lives with her Person
in NEW YORK,

a brother still in

...and the rest of my siblings are in museums all over the world.

AND ME...?

My Person lives part time in the
U.S. and part time in France,
so I travel quite a bit
and of course
we still do
concerts

and recordings...

My Maker was one of the best –
AND HE <u>TRAINED</u> SOME OF THE BEST:
Bücher, Reisinger, even a
young Maker named Martin
who took a ship to build
guitars in the *new* country.

Y**OU KNOW... THAT COMPANY
IS** *STILL* **MAKING GUITARS!**

MY GOODNESS!

My Maker invented the
steel rod
that goes through our necks
to keep them straight.

He invented
raised fingerboards
for a young Italian guitarist
named
Luigi Legnani

*(although I'm older
so I don't have that
kind of fingerboard)*

AND

my Maker
invented tuners with
GEARS

SO MY PERSON WOULDN'T HAVE TO
MUCK ABOUT WITH TUNING PEGS
LIKE ON A VIOLIN.

My Maker was *brilliant*
and he made hundreds of us…
but so few survived!

I was *9* years old when Napoléon attacked Vienna.

I was there.

LET ME TELL YOU, **THAT** WAS A TERRIFYING NIGHT!

You know, van Beethoven?

Old Ludwig had *idolized* Napoléon, but when the "LITTLE CORPORAL" declared himself Emperor, van Beethoven was so **furious,** that he destroyed the front page of his *Third Symphony* manuscript trying to erase his dedication of that piece to Napoléon!

Quite a character the Old Maestro was! a temper!

THEN A FEW YEARS LATER CAME THE ATTACK AND Beethoven ended up hiding in his basement to avoid the French cannons battering our city walls!

I suppose he was right about Napoléon — a common mortal — *a tyrant.*

It was fairly calm for a while, but then came your World War I. **My God.**

YOU CAN'T IMAGINE THE CARNAGE… *over 16 and a half million — DEAD.*

AND I SURVIVED IT.

I remember **Kristalnacht,**

"Crystal Night"
— that horrible evening back in 1938 when the Nazis
stormed through our neighborhood and broke out all the
storefront windows, leaving behind the tiny,
shattered pieces of glass
strewn all over the ground.

I REMEMBER THOSE PRISTINE SHARDS AT SUNRISE

like diamonds

quietly glistening in the morning light
with such a *terrified* innocence.

An innocence that couldn't *possibly*
foretell the horror that would
soon rape our continent

AND OUR MORALITY.

Then World War II —

when the Opera House down the street was so heavily bombed that you could see through the back wall,

past the stage and into the alley
and over 60 million more — DEAD.

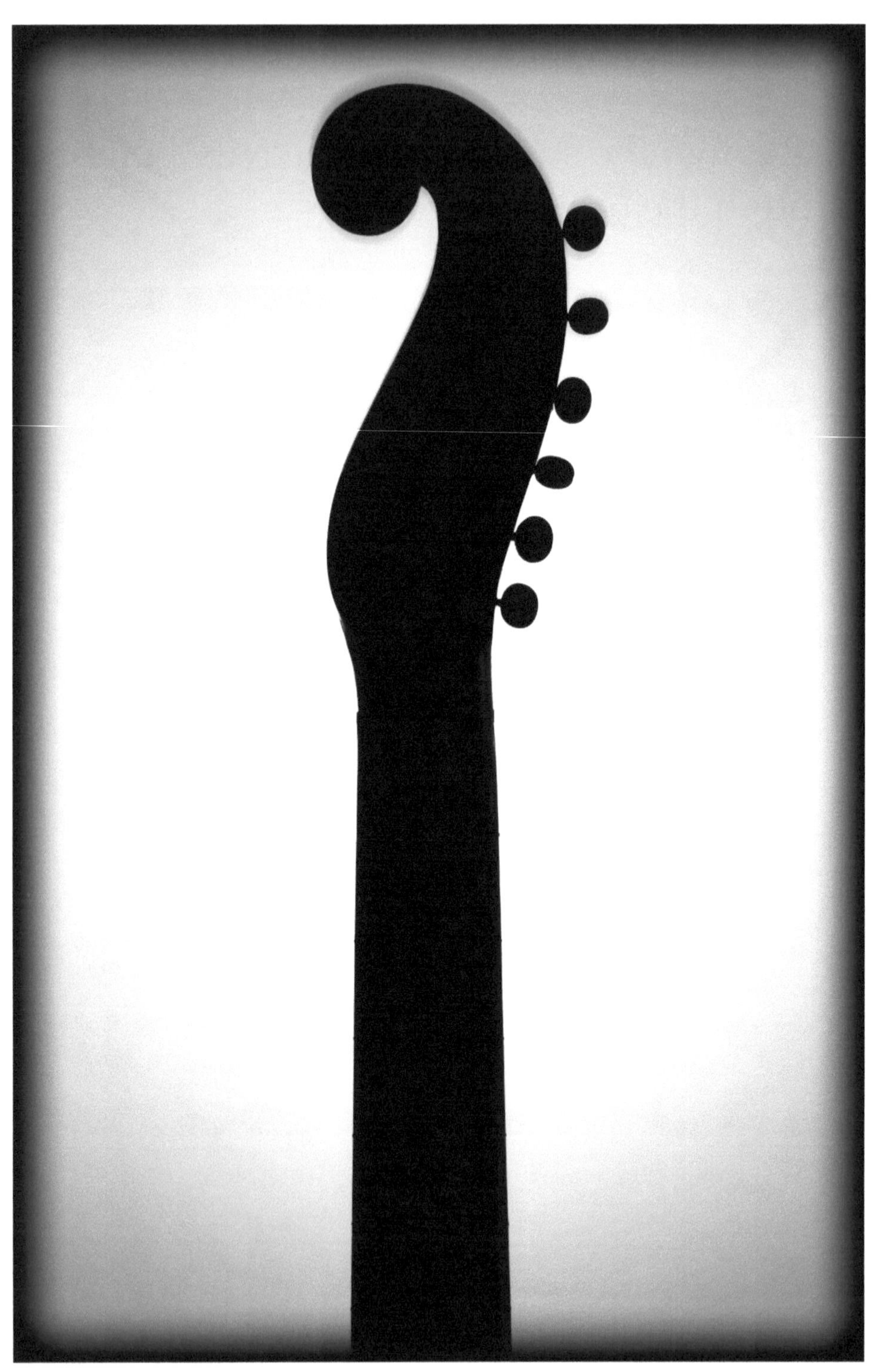

I survived that too,

and when my new Person found me on the wall of a shop in Vienna and took me to the United States, I survived that trip

even though the airline lost me for nearly a WEEK!

**I must say…
my new Person
was just about as furious
as Beethoven!**

Why did I survive and so many others didn't? WAS IT Mercy or Grace?

Mercy is when you don't get something BAD that you **_do_** deserve.

Grace is when you get something GOOD *that you **_don't_** deserve…*

THINK ABOUT THAT.

— *It wasn't Mercy* —

It was by **Grace** that I survived.

I didn't *deserve* it,
I didn't *earn* it,
and I can't account for
why *I* survived

and so many of my brothers and sisters *didn't.*

It was just a simple, *astounding*
act of Grace from the

Great Maker.

Recognizing that
IN EACH OF OUR LIVES…

maybe *Grace*
is what keeps us thankful,

NO?

MAYBE
it's what keeps us amazed
at the *miracle* of life!

REMEMBERING THAT

...isn't it also **Grace**
that keeps us *gentle*?

And Grace keeps us *KIND* —
even if we all,
somewhere
deep inside
— *just occasionally* —
can't avoid a touch of
what I've <u>ALWAYS</u> believed
is a **COMMON BOND** between us:

A SINFUL PRIDE that the **Great Maker**
gently forgives,

with a

knowing,

patient,

smile.

AFTER ALL -
YOU,
ME,
AND THE REST OF US…?

...WE'RE ONLY HUMAN.

I Speak — *Recording of Select Guitars from "I Speak" — Performed by Anthony Glise*

— CD Available Separately and as an Online Download —

TRACKS: RUN TIME:

1) **Anonymous** — *named "Constance"* (guitar born *ca.* 1814, Vienna, Austria [?]), performing: 9.34
Mauro Giuliani (1781-1829)
Grande Ouverture, Op. 61

2) **Gioachino Giussani** — *named "Sirius"* (guitar born 1996, Anghiari, Arezzo, Italy), performing: 7.06
Anthony Glise (*b.* 1956)
Theme and Variations on "Folias d'España," Op. 15

3) **Kenny Hill** — *named "Jayden"* (guitar born 2009, Ben Lomond, USA), performing: 3.59
Anthony Glise (*b.* 1956)
"Allegro" ("Woods' Run") from
Prelude, Fugue, & Allegro, "In the Eyes of the Wolf," Op. 31

4) **Franz Herzlieb, Sr.** — *named "Alma"* (guitar born *ca.* 1817, Graz, Austria), performing: 6.15
Fernando Sor (1778-1839)
Andante Largo, Op. 5, No. 5

5-7) **Gioachino Giussani** — *named "Eldamar"* (guitar born 1998, Anghiari, AZ, Italy), performing: 7.15
Anthony Glise (*b.* 1956)
Dream Scenes, Op. 9, A
  • *Rundtanz des Heinzelmännchen (Round Dance of the Little People)*
  • *Dryaden (Dryads)*
  • *Berggeister Spiele (Mountain Spirit Games)*

8-9) **José Ramírez** — *named "Diego Manuel Aurelio"* (guitar born 2008, Madrid, Spain), performing: 7.06
Francisco Tárrega (1852-1909)
  • *Lágrima*
  • *Capriccio Árabe*

10) **Hermann Hauser** — *named "Wilhelm"* (guitar born 1971, Munich, Germany), performing: 2.46
Francis Poulenc (1899-1963)
Sarabande, Op. 179 (1960)

11-13) **Johann Georg Staufer** — *named "Antonella"* (guitar born *ca.* 1800, Vienna, Austria), performing: 17.44
Anton Diabelli (1781-1858)
Sonata in F Major, Op. 29
  • *Allegro moderato* • *Andante sostenuto* • *Finale (Adagio, Presto)*

Total Run Time: 61.25

WHEN I PLAY A GUITAR, I'm playing a guitar *AND* I'm having a conversation with a dear friend, and if you happen to be around and eavesdrop when we're doing all that, it's usually called
"A Concert."
Anyone who thinks playing a guitar is merely "playing a guitar" diminishes reality.
How <u>sad</u> for those who hear only the SOUND!
— Anthony

1) Anonymous — named "Constance"
(guitar born *ca.* 1814, Vienna, Austria [?]),
performing: Mauro Giuliani (1781-1829) —
Grande Ouverture, Op. 61

CONSTANCE HAD THIS TO SAY ABOUT SINGING THE *GRANDE OUVERTURE*:
"I've always loved the *Grande Ouverture!* I remember when I first sang it in my Maker's shop (I think it might have been Giuliani himself who stopped by to try me out after I was born - I really don't recall). This piece has the power, depth, and emotion that we respected so much back in old Vienna!"

2) Gioachino Giussani — named "Sirius"
(guitar born 1996, Anghiari, Arezzo, Italy),
performing: Anthony Glise (*b.* 1956) —
Theme & Variations on "Folias d'España," Op. 15

SIRIUS HAD THIS TO SAY ABOUT SINGING MY *THEME AND VARIATIONS ON FOLIAS DE ESPAÑA*:
"Anthony's *Variations on 'Folias de España'* is one of hundreds composed on this theme since its emergence in the 15th century. Virtually every composer has written a set of variations on this theme but Anthony's set is unique in that it expands the harmonic, melodic, and formal structure of the theme. Virtuosic, contemporary, and beautiful, it has become one of his best known works for solo classical guitar."

3) Kenny Hill — named "Jayden"
(guitar born 2009, Ben Lomond, USA),
performing: Anthony Glise (*b.* 1956) —
"Allegro" ("Woods' Run") from *Prelude, Fugue, & Allegro, "In the Eyes of the Wolf," Op. 31*

JAYDEN HAD THIS TO SAY ABOUT PERFORMING *WOODS' RUN*:
"I'm the youngest of all the guitars on this CD - a teenager in your human years - so it's an honor to be on this CD with all these famous old dudes! I like singing pieces with a **LOT** of energy! Eventually I'll be old enough to sing some of these other pieces, but for now… MAN - it's just cool to PLAY (and I guess show off a little) and this piece is just perfect for me! *PS* - If you have a chance, please write Anthony and tell him you'd like to hear me sing some Bach. He keeps saying I'm too young, but I'm pretty sure I can handle it!"

FROM ANTHONY: "Woods' Run" IS THE "ALLEGRO" from my *Prelude, Fugue, and Allegro* (titled *In The Eyes of the Wolf*). To explain, several years ago I had the honor of holding an Artist-in-Residence at the Standing Rock Sioux Indian Reservation (the final resting place of murdered Lakota Sioux Holy Man, Húŋkešni ["Sitting Bull"]), and to integrate me into the community, the tribal council held a "Sweat Lodge" (purification rite) for me.

With the extreme heat and sensory deprivation, after several hours, participants often begin to hallucinate and are visited by their "Animal Spirit." That spirit (which can be one of many different animals) will talk and advise you on different aspects of life and will visit you unannounced throughout the rest of your life.
In the Eyes of the Wolf is about that first conversation.

4) Franz Herzlieb, Sr. — named "Alma"
(guitar born *ca.* 1817, Graz, Austria),
performing: Fernando Sor (1778-1839) —
Andante Largo, Op. 5, No. 5

ALMA SAID THAT SHE LOVES THIS PIECE BECAUSE:
"I just love it. It's sort of MY business why... *now isn't it?"*

5-7) Gioachino Giussani — named "Eldamar"
(guitar born 1998, Anghiari, AZ, Italy),
performing: Anthony Glise (*b.* 1956) —
Dream Scenes, Op. 9, A
- *Rundtanz des Heinzelmännchen (Round Dance of the Little People)*
- *Dryaden (Dryads)*
- *Berggeister Spiele (Mountain Spirit Games)*

ELDAMAR HAD THIS TO SAY ABOUT PERFORMING MY *DREAM SCENES*:
"I am a <u>PURE</u> concert guitar, so I naturally have different reasons for what I like to sing than some of these other guitars. I'm also Italian so *(I suppose)* I can be just a little bit opinionated, but, *vedete, non c'e' problema?!* I don't **<u>CARE!</u>** *Dream Scenes* is a great concert piece. It's perfectly composed, highly 'visual,' and I enjoy programmatic pieces. If you don't - *you should.* What could be more fun than Anthony's brilliant musical representation of the different Austrian elves that he has met through the years? *Eh?!"*

FROM ANTHONY: ELDAMAR HAS ALWAYS ENJOYED playing **Dream Scenes** ["Traum Szenen" in German], especially because he likes the story behind this piece. For that reason *(just to keep him happy)* I thought the background might be worth recounting.

I composed *Dream Scenes* around *Johannesnacht (Midsummer's Night)* in Vienna, 1995, inspired by a series of dreams that haunted me for over a week.

Each movement depicts different Austrian elves in their natural surroundings: the playful barbarism of the *Rundtanz der Heinzelmännchen* ("Round Dance of the Little People"), the graceful *Dryaden* ("Tree Spirits") and the antics of *Berggeister Spiele* ("Mountain Spirit Games").*

**Here I mean specifically Birch and Willow tree spirits. Oak or Walnut spirits (at least those I have met) lack the grace conveyed in this movement.*

**8-9) José Ramírez — named "Diego Manuel Aurelio"
(guitar born 2008, Madrid, Spain),**
performing: Francisco Tárrega (1852-1909) —
- *Lágrima*
- *Capriccio Árabe*

DIEGO HAD THIS TO SAY ABOUT SINGING TARREGA'S WORKS:

"I'm from one of the oldest families of guitar makers founded by José Ramírez in Madrid back in 1890. Tárrega has *just* as much lineage **and lineage is a strange thing:** we try our entire lives to break away from it in order to be "ourselves," yet it's the lineage itself that unavoidably defines us. I *love* these works (and, I must say, I sing them very well), but one of my greatest joys was to have *Señora Amelia Ramírez* (now, the director of our family guitar shop in Madrid) send us such a kind note from Madrid on the advent of this book. **LINEAGE…!** We must never forget from whence we descend! Honor is *everything* and we owe that honor to our forefathers who helped us ALL become who we are today!"

**10) Hermann Hauser — named "Wilhelm"
(guitar born 1971, Munich, Germany),**
performing: Francis Poulenc (1899-1963) —
Sarabande, Op. 179

WILHELM HAD THIS TO SAY ABOUT PERFORMING THE SARABANDE:

"As an old German, it was a *pleasure* to play such an emotional French composition! Almost never recorded, Poulenc's *Sarabande* allowed me to show off the extreme timbres and articulation for which all Hauser guitars are famous."

**11-13) Johann Georg Staufer — named "Antonella"
(guitar born *ca.* 1800, Vienna, Austria),**
performing: Anton Diabelli (1781-1858) —
Sonata in F Major, Op. 29
- *Allegro moderato*
- *Andante sostenuto*
- *Finale (Adagio, Presto)*

ANTONELLA HAD THIS TO SAY ABOUT SINGING DIABELLI'S SONATA IN F MAJOR:

"Well now… Anthony and I have worked together for over 35 years but I have to say, singing Diabelli's *Sonata in F* was a special treat. You know, I was in Vienna when Diabelli wrote that piece! He lived a few streets over from my Maker's shop, which was just around the corner from where Beethoven lived (in the Ballgasse), and down the street from where old Mozart died. My *goodness*, that seems like a long time ago!"

"Oh - it was *also* just a few blocks from *Café Frauenhuber,* over on Himmelpfortgasse—they have been around since 1824 and they have the <u>BEST</u> Mohnschnitten (a little poppy-seed cake) and - *OH* - it was just a few blocks from *Café Hawelka* (I *always* loved their coffee - if you go there, you HAVE to try their *'Melange'* - it's sort of like Italian *cappuccino*, but with chocolate sprinkled on top and a lot more foam—and be SURE to get their *Apple Strüdel*—oh,

and across the street from Café Hawelka they have those little sandwiches! You know, Franz Kafka used to eat lunch there! He especially liked the little finger sandwiches with thin-sliced beef and just a touch of fresh horseradish on the side — *now that's true!* That's even in his biography, you know?"

"Anyway, I truly enjoyed singing on this CD and having my portrait taken by Megan *(what a nice young lady she is!)* and I'm sure you'll enjoy this CD, the book, *I Speak,* and visiting the gallery exhibition of *I Speak.* All wonderful photos, music — *and about our interviews…?* Well, we *finally* got a chance to *talk,* you know?! But now you remember, the next time you're in Vienna, you really *must* visit *Café Frauenhubner!"*

"You just tell them that I sent you, *OK?"*

*With a Warm Embrace
to Every One of You!*

Antonella

---

production & engineering on this recording by:
Thomas Ransom
—Ransomed Productions
all strings (gut, nylon, & recording) by:
— E&O Mari - LaBella
microphones by:
— Audio-Technica

ANTHONY IS UNDER CONTRACT TO, AND PROUDLY ENDORSES:
Microphones: Audio Technica (US)
Strings: E&O Mari—LaBella (New York, US)
Cedar-top ClassicalGuitars: Paul Jacobson (US)
Steel String Guitars and Strings: C.F. Martin (US)
Amplifiers: Marshall Amplification, Ltd. (England)
Electric/nylon-string Synth Guitars: Godin (Canada)
Spruce-top Classical Guitars: Gioachino Guissani, (Arezzo, Italy)

MEGAN WYETH has studied with many

celebrated photographers including Ansel Adams, Arnold Newman, and Morley Baer. Her formal background includes photography study at the *Kansas City Art Institute* and a degree in art history from the *University of Kansas*.

Blessed with a deep love of nature, Megan and her husband own a small farm in Missouri, teeming with regional wildlife (including a posse of wild turkeys), a grove of walnut trees, and an adult tree house.

Megan has maintained an active studio, gallery exhibition, and publishing schedule for over 30 years. Her works are currently held in numerous private and public collections internationally.

An almost mystical approach to the subject matter gives her works an astounding sense of depth, motion, and personality.

In her own words,

"As we look through the lens, we see shapes, forms, light, value, and color—and we begin to arrange these elements; intuition takes over and that quiet, inner awareness, transforms into a picture."

"I think of this process as exploring, or 'opening doors,' as each subject presents itself. The photographer has the humble responsibility to document that fleeting moment of honesty."

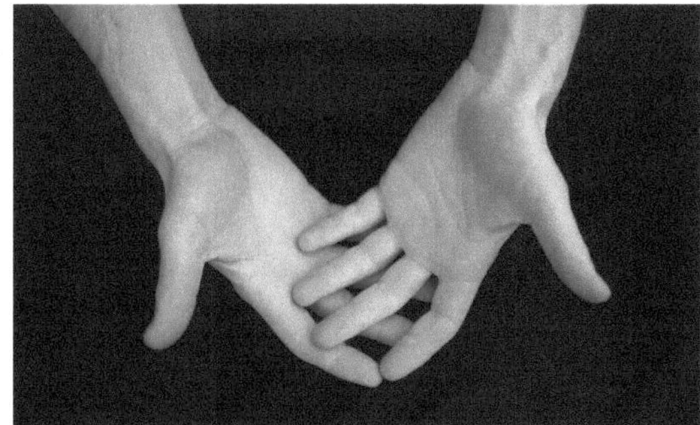

ANTHONY GLISE is a concert and record-

ing artist, composer, and author. He lives part-time in France, and part-time in the US. Anthony has previously held full-time teaching posts in Austria, Germany, France, Italy, and the US.

A composer and board member of the *French Film Commission*, Anthony frequently performs with select musicians of the *French National Orchestra-Lille*, and was one of five international scholars selected for the panel of *The Soundboard Scholar*, a peer-reviewed journal published by the world's largest classical guitar organization, *The Guitar Foundation of America*.

Anthony is the only US-born classical guitarist to win First Prize at the *International Toscanini Competition* (Italy) and his concerts, CDs, books, and compositions have consistently received 5-star reviews worldwide. His past concert venues include *Carnegie Hall*, *Lincoln Center* (US), *Vienna International Center* (Austria), *Nouveau Siècle* (of the French National Orchestra-Lille), *etc.*

He has earned nine diplomas from seven countries including study at *New England Conservatory* and *Harvard University* (US), *Accademia degli Studi "L'Ottocento"* (Italy), *Konservatorium der Stadt* (Vienna, Austria), and *Université Catholique* (France), as well as European diplomas in French and German languages.

Anthony is also a licensed Emergency Medical Technician, a university fencing coach, and *(when life permits)* he hides quietly on his 7 meter, cutter-rigged sailboat, christened *Gargoyle II*.

In Europe, Anthony lives *(on land)* in the tiny idyllic village of Sainghin-en-Mélantois, in Northern France where,

"... WE HAVE 600 PEOPLE, 900 COWS, 2 CAFÉS, AND THE NEWEST CHURCH IN THE AREA...

BUILT IN 1568."